A THOUSAND THEOS

by Lori Haskins Houran
Illustrated by Amy Wummer

Kane Press
New York

For the real Jordan. Thanks for the great idea!—LHH

To our beloved family pets: Beau, Rocky, Flint, and Zuzu—AW

Acknowledgments: We wish to thank the following people for their helpful advice and review of the material contained in this book: Susan Longo, Early Childhood and Elementary School Teacher, Mamaroneck, NY; and Rebeka Eston Salemi, Kindergarten Teacher, Lincoln School, Lincoln, MA.

Special thanks to Susan Longo for providing the Activities That Matter in the back of this book.

Text copyright © 2015 by Lori Haskins Houran
Illustrations copyright © 2015 by Amy Wummer

Library of Congress Cataloging-in-Publication Data

Houran, Lori Haskins.
  A thousand Theos / by Lori Haskins Houran ; illustrated by Amy Wummer.
    pages cm. — (Math matters)
  Summary: Introduces the math concept of doubling as Jordan enlists the help of her friends to find a lost puppy.
  ISBN 978-1-57565-803-2 (pbk. : alk. paper)
  [1. Lost and found possessions—Fiction. 2. Dogs—Fiction. 3. Addition—Fiction.] I. Wummer, Amy, illustrator. II. Title.
  PZ7.H27645Th 2015
  [E]—dc23
                          2015013899
eISBN: 978-1-57565-804-9

10 9 8 7 6 5 4 3 2

Kane Press

An imprint of Boyds Mills & Kane, a division of Astra Publishing House

www.kanepress.com

Printed in China

Math Matters is a registered trademark of Astra Publishing House

"Jordan, have you seen my puppy?"

Jordan looked down at her neighbor Benny. He was usually bouncy and happy—kind of like a puppy himself! But not today.

"I haven't seen him," said Jordan. "Is he lost?"

Benny nodded. "See?"

Jordan read the sign Benny's mom was taping to the front door.

"Can't we look for him now?" Benny begged his mom.

"I'm so sorry, honey—we have to go," she said. "But I bet someone will see your sign and find him."

"It's just one little sign," said Benny in a shaky voice.

"I'll make another one," Jordan offered. "I can hang it up at the soccer field on my way to practice."

"That would be great!" said Benny's mom. "Oh, here's our bus. Come on, Benny."

"Don't worry," Jordan told him. "We'll find Theo!"

Jordan ran upstairs.

She took out her markers and copied Benny's sign. She added bright red stars in the corners to make it stand out.

I wish I could do more to help, she thought. Still, two signs were twice as good as one.

Benny
↓
Jordan

1 + 1 = 2

Jordan was putting up her sign when Cora and Carl rode by on their bikes.

"What's up?" asked Cora.

"Cute dog!" said Carl.

Jordan told them about Benny's lost puppy.

"Benny was worried that one sign wasn't enough. So I made a second one," Jordan explained.

"Poor little guy!" said Cora. "I'll make a sign."

"Me too," said Carl. "That will double the signs to four."

Hmm, thought Jordan. *Double.* That gave her an idea.

Benny
↓
Jordan
↙   ↘
Cora   Carl

2 + 2 = 4

"Do you think you could each get two more friends to make signs?" asked Jordan. "That would double the number again—to eight."

"Cool!" said Cora.

"We're on it!" said Carl.

Jordan felt much better. Eight signs—that was pretty good! Maybe somebody would see one and find Theo. Benny would be so happy!

Cora and Carl made their signs right away.
Cora tacked hers up at the skateboard park,
where she ran into Mack and Abby. They
wanted to make signs too.

Carl stapled his sign on the library bulletin board. He told Evan and Leena (very quietly!) what was going on. They couldn't wait to make signs of their own.

Soon there were eight Lost Dog signs hanging up around town.

Benny
↓
Jordan
Cora   Carl
Mack   Abby   Evan   Leena

4 + 4 = 8

But it didn't stop there. Everyone who made a sign asked two *more* kids to make one.

Mack asked his neighbors Nick and Andy.

8 + 8 = 16

Abby asked her teammates Riley and Sam.

Evan asked his cousins Tyler and Brett.

Leena asked her best friends, Carrie and Fiona.

The word kept spreading. The signs kept doubling!

By lunchtime, there were signs at Pirate Pizza, Joy's Toys, and The Awesome Blossom.

$$16 + 16 = 32$$
$$32 + 32 = 64$$
$$64 + 64 = 128$$

By dinnertime, there were
signs at Bowl-a-Bunch, Mike's
Bikes, and The Book Nook.
And still . . .

. . . the signs kept doubling, until every kid in town had made one!

Jordan couldn't believe it. Theo's face was everywhere! Someone *had* to find him now, didn't they?

128 + 128 = 256
256 + 256 = 512
512 + 512 = 1,024

21

"Jordan! Jordan!" called Benny, running up the sidewalk. "Look at all the Theos! There must be a hundred of them!"

"I think it's more like a thousand," said his mom.

"A thousand Theos!" Benny yelped. "Did you make them all?"

Jordan shook her head.

"I only made one. Then two friends made them. They each asked two friends, and *they* each asked two friends, and . . . well, it turns out doubling works fast!"

"Wow!" said Benny.

Then his smile faded.

"But . . . the *real* Theo is still gone."

Benny sat down on the steps. His mom and Jordan sat beside him.

DING! DING! DING!

Benny didn't even look up at the sound of the ice cream truck. Jordan watched it pull in front of their building.

"Hi there," the ice cream man said. "I was going to call, but I decided to stop by since you're right on my route. Is this guy yours?" He held up a wiggly brown puppy.

"THEO!" cried Benny.

The puppy jumped from the man's arms and ran straight to Benny. Benny hugged him tightly.

"Where did you find him?" Benny asked.

"Way on the other side of town. I saw all the signs and figured this had to be Theo. Though I offered him a lick of peanut butter ice cream just to be sure."

"Thank you so much!" said Benny.

"You're welcome!" said the ice cream man. "Would you kids like some ice cream, too?"

"Oooh—yes, please!" Benny picked peanut butter to share with Theo. Jordan chose cherry vanilla with sprinkles.

The ice cream man pulled away, tooting his
horn cheerfully.

"Thanks again!" Benny called after him.

"Woof!" added Theo.

"Thank you, too, Jordan," said Benny's mom.
"But how are we ever going to thank all the
other people who made signs?"

"Easy," said Jordan. She grinned. "Just thank one person and ask them to thank two more. If you use doubling, you'll have a thousand thanks in no time!"

DOUBLING CHART

Jordan is right. Doubling works fast! Start with the number one and double it. Keep on doubling, and you'll pass 1,000 in just ten steps.

$1 + 1 = 2$

$2 + 2 = 4$

$4 + 4 = 8$

$8 + 8 = 16$

$16 + 16 = 32$

$32 + 32 = 64$

$64 + 64 = 128$

$128 + 128 = 256$

$256 + 256 = 512$

$512 + 512 = 1,024$